DAX AND THE DUNES

Written by Jenny Phillips

Illustrated by Tanya Glebova

© 2019 Jenny Phillips
www.goodandbeautiful.com

CHAPTER 1

The car came to a stop, and Dax jumped out.

"The dunes!" he sang. "I am at the dunes!"

Last year Dax read a book. In the book a boy visited the

dunes. "I want to go, too!" Dax said.

"Yes," said Dad. "We will save up and go next year."

All year Dax dreamed

of the dunes. He read the book to his little sister, Jill.

At last the trip had come.

They drove a long, long time. Now they were at the dunes.

Dax looked at the big hills of sand and was so glad to be there.

"Come on, Jill. Let's go to the top of the tallest hill," said Dax.

At the top they looked far and wide. They were by the sea. It was long and blue.

Dax and Jill saw Dad setting up the tent. They wanted to help. The kids

jumped, hopped, and slid down the hill. Wheeeeeee!

The tent was up, and lunch was done. It was time to explore. Mom,

Dad, Dax, and Jill set off.

They came to a hill with a

small dune. It was a great spot to jump. It was the

best spot to jump.

Dax and Jill glided in the breeze and landed in the soft sand.

The birds came to see, and they agreed; it was the best spot to jump.

The kids were tired and needed a rest.

In a clump of trees, they sat and ate lunch. Dax loved the shade and the sweet-smelling blossoms

on the sand.

"Look," said Dad very softly. "In those trees over

there, I see a red fox. You will not see that often. It is rare to see red foxes because they often sleep in the day. They make their

dens in the dunes and eat birds, eggs, and fish."

"That's so neat," said Dax.

"The fox is cute," said Jill.

CHAPTER 2

The next day, rays of sun shone on the tent. It was the day to go to the beach.

"Are there sharks?" asked Jill as they ate.

"No," said Dad.

"Can a big wave get me?" asked Jill.

"No," said Mom.

They packed their things and walked on the path to the beach.

"Will a big crab bite me?" Jill asked.

"No!" said Mom and Dad.

Dax dashed to the waves. He let his feet get wet as the waves rolled in.

He saw a seagull glide.

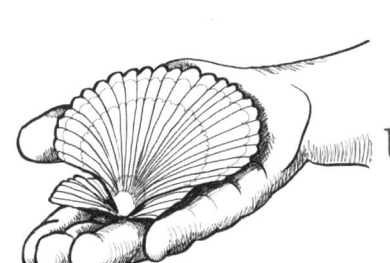

He picked up a shell.

He saw a ship in the mist.

He saw rocks rise up, up, up.

Then he saw Jill. She sat way up on the sand. She was not running or having fun.

"Come on, Jill! Come get

wet!" yelled Dax.

"No," said Jill. "I do not want to get slime on me from seaweed. I do not like sharks or crabs."

Sharks, crabs, slime? Jill was scared, and Dax wanted to help her. He said a prayer in his mind for Jill and sat by her side.

"You must try not to be scared," he said. "Let me help you."

Dax got a small bit of seaweed and asked Jill to feel it.

"It's not too bad, is it?"

"No, it is not," agreed Jill.

Dax took Jill's hand. "Let's walk to the water—not too far, just so you can feel a wave on your feet."

"Let's look for shells," said Dax.

"No," said Jill. "A crab will pinch me."

"The crabs on this beach are so small that they are scared of you. They will run from you. Trust me."

"Okay," said Jill, and they looked for shells.

Jill spun in the wind.

She chased a seagull.

She let waves swish on her feet.

She hugged Dax.

"Thank you for helping me not be scared!"

The two kids played all day. Jill let Dad take her far into the water in his arms, and Dax swam like a fish.

Mom splashed and dove.

The seagulls came to see it all.

CHAPTER 3

Three days had passed. It was time to go home. Dad let the kids go to the top of the tallest dune one more time.

Dax sat with a prayer in his heart. "I thank Thee, God, for the swell of waves."

"I thank Thee for the fresh smell of salt. I thank Thee for family to share it all with me."

Years and years went by. Dax was now a dad. His son picked up a book from the shelf. It was the same book Dax had read as a boy—the book about the dunes.

"Dad!" said the boy. "Can we go to the dunes?"

"Yes," said Dax. "We will save up and go next year."

All year the boy dreamed of the dunes. He read the book to his little sister. You can guess the rest . . .

The End